D1221109

To: _____

From: _____

"Therefore encourage one another
and build one another up,
just as you are doing."
—1 Thessalonians 5:11

Copyright © 2023 by Berenstain Publishing, Inc. All rights reserved. Published in the United States by Random House Children's Books, a division of Penguin Random House LLC, New York. Random House and the colophon are registered trademarks of Penguin Random House LLC.

Visit us on the Web!
rhcbooks.com
BerenstainBears.com

Educators and librarians, for a variety of teaching tools, visit us at RHTeachersLibrarians.com

Library of Congress Control Number: 2022937957
ISBN 978-0-593-30256-9 (trade) — ISBN 978-0-593-30528-7 (ebook)

MANUFACTURED IN CHINA
10 9 8 7 6 5 4 3 2 1

Random House Children's Books supports the First Amendment and celebrates the right to read.

Penguin Random House LLC supports copyright. Copyright fuels creativity, encourages diverse voices, promotes free speech, and creates a vibrant culture. Thank you for buying an authorized edition of this book and for complying with copyright laws by not reproducing, scanning, or distributing any part in any form without permission. You are supporting writers and allowing Penguin Random House to publish books for every reader.

The Berenstain Bears.
Gifts of the Spirit
Helping

Mike Berenstain

Based on the characters created by
Stan and Jan Berenstain

Random House 🏠 New York

Mama, Papa, and the cubs were all kept very busy taking care of their tree house home. So Mama didn't have much time for hobbies. But she did make time for a very special hobby—quilting. She was one of the best quilters in all of Bear Country. Her quilts were beautiful! In fact, she was president of the Bear Country Quilters Club.

Not only that, but she had also turned her hobby into a business when she opened her own quilt shop. It was a lot of work running a business and doing daily chores, too. Mama made it work, though!

It happened that the Quilters Club was planning an outing. They wanted to go to the Quilters Convention in Big Bear City. That would mean an overnight trip—not something Mama had done on her own in many years. Mama was a little worried about it.

"I would like to go on this overnight trip to the Quilters Convention," she sighed to Papa. "I would so love to see all the quilts on display and meet with other quilters."

"Sounds great to me!" replied Papa. "What's to stop you?"

"What's to stop me?" said Mama. "Who's going to take care of my share of the chores while I'm gone—all the cooking, cleaning, and shopping I take on around here?"

"Why, yours truly, Papa Q. Bear, of course," said Papa proudly. "The cubs and I are great at chores. We'll do it all. We can handle the job with one hand tied behind our backs!"

"Oh, is that so?" replied Mama. "Well, we'll see about that!"

Just then, the phone rang. It was the vice president of the Quilters Club.

"Yes," said Mama into the phone. "I've been thinking it over, and I will definitely be going to the convention!"

"Way to go!" said Papa.

"As for things here at home," said Mama, "I'll just do what I can before I leave and hope for the best."

"Bye, Mama!" called the cubs as she drove away in the family car. "And don't worry!" shouted Papa. "We can handle things here! No problem!"

Papa got right to work.
"First," he said, "I'm going
to clean all these rugs."
"We'll get the vacuum
cleaner," said the cubs.

"Never mind!" said
Papa. "I'm going to get
the deep-down dirt out
with an old-fashioned
rug beater!"

He snatched up the rugs and ran out the door.

"Uh-oh!" said the cubs. They remembered that Mama had just put the wash on the line.

Whack! Whack! Whack! went the rug beater. Clouds of dirt billowed from the rugs.

"Stop, Papa! Stop!" said the cubs. "All that dirt is getting on Mama's clean washing!"

"Never mind!" said Papa. "It will surely rain, and the dirt will rinse off before Mama gets home!"

"Now you cubs are in for a real treat," said Papa. "It's time for lunch. I'm going to make my triple-flip honey-mustard pancakes!"

"Honey mustard?" said the cubs, making faces.

Papa began flipping pancakes. But on his third flip, he got a little carried away and flipped a pancake so high that it stuck to the ceiling.

"Never mind!" said Papa, scraping the gooey mess off the ceiling and serving it to the cubs. "Mama's ceiling is clean enough to eat off!"

"Now," said Papa after lunch, "how about a cozy fire in the fireplace?"

"Don't forget to open the chimney!" shouted the cubs as Papa lit the fire. Since the smoke couldn't go out of the closed chimney, it billowed back into the house.

"Never mind!" said Papa, trying to beat the fire out with a pillow. But the pillow burst open, and clouds of feathers flew everywhere.

The cubs brought buckets of water from the kitchen and doused the fire. It steamed and hissed as dirty water ran onto the floor.

Oh, no! thought the cubs.
What a mess! Smoke!

Feathers!

Wet gunk in the fireplace!

Pancake goo on the ceiling!

Dirty wash on the line!

That's when the phone rang. It was Mama. It turned out that the Quilters Convention had been canceled because of a power outage. So Mama was starting for home and would arrive soon.

"Papa," said Brother, "what can we do to help?"

"I think I'm beyond help," said Papa.

"Nonsense!" said spunky Sister Bear. "You're never beyond help—not when you have helpful cubs like us around! Come, Brother! Come, Honey!"

The cubs went to work like three little whirlwinds.

Sister blew smoke out the window with a fan. Brother mopped the dirty floor. Honey vacuumed feathers, and all three rinsed the dirty wash in the brook at the bottom of the hill. Before you could say "triple-flip honey-mustard pancakes," everything was tidied up and put away.

Then Mama arrived home.

After hugging Papa and the cubs, she looked around in surprise.

"The house looks wonderful, my dear!" she said. "However did you do it?"

"Well," said Papa, "I admit it was more work than I expected. But I had a *little* help from my three assistants here!"

Papa smiled at the cubs.

"Yes!" they agreed, smiling back. "Just a *little*!"